THE FABULOUS LOST & FOUND

AND THE LITTLE UKRAINIAN MOUSE

WRITTEN BY MARK PALLIS
ILLUSTRATED BY PETER BAYNTON

NEU WESTEND
— PRESS —

For Stepan, Natalia and Oliver - MP

For Hannah and Skye - PB

THE FABULOUS LOST & FOUND AND THE LITTLE UKRAINIAN MOUSE

First Printing, 2020
ISBN: 978-1-913595-12-8
NeuWestendPress.com

THE FABULOUS LOST & FOUND

AND THE LITTLE UKRAINIAN MOUSE

WRITTEN BY MARK PALLIS
ILLUSTRATED BY PETER BAYNTON

NEU WESTEND
— PRESS —

In the middle of the big city is a tiny
yellow building. If anyone loses anything, this is
where it ends up.

It is called the Lost and Found.

Mr and Mrs Frog keep everything safe, hoping that someday every lost watch and bag and phone and toy and shoe and cheesegrater will find its owner again.

But the shop is very small. And there are so many lost things. It is all quite a squeeze, but still, it's fabulous.

One sunny day, a little mouse walked in.

"Welcome," said Mrs Frog. "What have you lost?"

"Я загубила свою шапку," said the mouse.

Mr and Mrs Frog could not speak Ukrainian. They had no idea what the little mouse was saying.

What shall we do? they wondered.

Maybe she's lost an umbrella. Everyone loses an umbrella at least twice, thought Mr Frog.

"Have you lost this?" asked Mr Frog.

"Парасольку? Hi," replied the mouse.

Then Mrs Frog remembered something
that had been handed in a few months ago...

"Is this yours?" Mrs Frog asked, holding up a chunk of cheese.

"Сир? Ні. Він смердить!" said the mouse.

"Time to put that cheese in the bin dear," said Mr Frog.

"Maybe the word 'шапка' means coat," said Mr Frog.

"Now where did I put that nice
yellow one?"

"Got it!" said Mr Frog.

"Пальто? Hi. Я загубила свою шапку,"
said the mouse.

She was starting to feel a bit frustrated.

"We need to keep trying," said Mrs Frog.

Не шарф.

Не штани.

Не светр.

Не сонцезахисні окуляри.

Не туфлі.

"Я загубила свою шапку," said the mouse.

Не два велосипеди.

Не комп'ютер.

Не три книги.

Не чотири банани.

Не п'ять ключів.

It was no good. A fat wet tear rolled
down the mouse's cheek.

"How about a nice cup of tea?" asked Mrs Frog kindly.

"Я люблю чай. Дякую," replied the mouse.
They sat together, sipping their tea and all feeling a bit sad.

Suddenly, the mouse realised she could try pointing.

"Шапка!" she said.

"I've got it!" exclaimed Mrs Frog, leaping up.

"A wig of course!" said Mrs Frog.

"Не перуку," said the mouse.

Не червону.

Не світлу.

Не коричневу.

Не різнокольорову.

Не зелену.

"What about this?"
asked Mr Frog, pulling back
a curtain.

"Так!" exclaimed the
mouse.

Занадто маленький.

Занадто великий.

Занадто високий.

Занадто вузький.

"One hat left," said
Mrs Frog, reaching all
the way to the back of the
cupboard.

"It couldn't be this
old thing, could it?"

"Моя шапка. Я знайшла свою шапку! Велике дякую,"

said the mouse.

"Ah, so 'шапка' means hat. Wonderful!"
Mr and Mrs Frog smiled.

And just like that, the mouse found her hat.

"До побачення," she said, as she skipped away.
"До побачення," replied Mr and Mrs Frog.

"I wonder who will come tomorrow?" said Mr Frog.
Mrs Frog put her arm around him.

"I don't know," she replied, giving him a squeeze,
"but whoever it is, we'll do our best to help."

LEARNING TO LOVE LANGUAGES

An additional language opens a child's mind, broadens their horizons and enriches their emotional life. Research has shown that the time between a child's birth and their sixth or seventh birthday is a "golden period" when they are most receptive to new languages. This is because they have an in-built ability to distinguish the sounds they hear and make sense of them. The Story-powered Language Learning Method taps into these natural abilities.

HOW THE STORY-POWERED LANGUAGE LEARNING METHOD WORKS

We create an emotionally engaging and funny story for children and adults to enjoy together, just like any other picture book. Studies show that social interaction, like enjoying a book together, is critical in language learning.

Through the story, we introduce a relatable character who speaks only in the new language. This helps build empathy and a positive attitude towards people who speak different languages. These are both important aspects in laying the foundations for lasting language acquisition in a child's life.

As the story progresses, the child naturally works with the characters to discover the meanings of a wide range of fun new words. Strategic use of humour ensures that this subconscious learning is rewarded with laughter; the child feels good and the first seeds of a lifelong love of languages are sown.

For more information and free downloads visit www.neuwestendpress.com

я загубила свою шапку	I've lost my hat
парасолька	umbrella
сир	cheese
він смердить	it stinks
пальто	coat
шарф	scarf
штани	trousers
сонцезахисні окуляри	sunglasses
светр	sweater
туфлі	shoes
один	one
два	two
три	three
чотири	four
п'ять	five
комп'ютер	computer
книга	book
ключ	key
банан	banana
велосипед	bicycle
я люблю чай	I love tea
дякую	thank you
перука	wig
червона	red
світла	blond
коричнева	brown
зелена	green
різнокольорова	multicoloured
шапка	hat
занадто високий	too tall
занадто великий	too big
занадто маленький	too small
занадто вузький	too tight
я знайшла свою шапку	I've found my hat
Велике дякую	thank you very much
до побачення	goodbye

THE WORLD OF
THE FABULOUS LOST & FOUND

THIS STORY IS ALSO AVAILABLE IN...

FRENCH
RUSSIAN
ITALIAN
CZECH
WELSH
KOREAN
GERMAN
HEBREW
SWEDISH
POLISH
CHINESE
VIETNAMESE
LATIN
PORTUGUESE

...AND MANY MORE LANGUAGES!

ENJOYED IT?
WRITE A REVIEW AND
LET US KNOW!

@MARK_PALLIS ON TWITTER
WWW.MARKPALLIS.COM

@PETERBAYNTON ON INSTAGRAM
WWW.PETERBAYNTON.COM

Printed in Great Britain
by Amazon